# I'm a
# Winner

By Michael Alonzo Williams

Tellwell Talent
www.tellwell.ca

ISBN
978-0-2288-5808-9 (Paperback)
978-0-2288-5809-6 (eBook)

# Table of Contents

# Chapter 1

# Cupcake Challenge

"Just one more," sighed Lars Pushkin in enchantment as he stretched his overworked jaws to complete that last bite, totaling a dozen cupcakes during the entire sitting.

Lars is a 12-year-old boy who lives with the battle of overeating. In his battle, a subconscious villain has manifested as a character named Mr. 'T'—short for Mr. Temptation. Mr. Temptation appears as a tall, thin figure adorned with a narrow-brim hat and a dark trench coat. He comes across as a subconsciously spooky dude. Even worse is what he has hidden underneath his trench coat.

By now Lars' stomach was again in pain, for he had chowed down far too many cupcakes. Unfortunately, it has been an ongoing battle. His lack of self-esteem as left him at a disadvantage. Standing 4'7" and 85 pounds, you could say Lars was a well-rounded kid. He's a bit overweight and he knows it. Obesity hinders him in everything he does. Right now it is tough being a kid.

Lars resides in a cozy little cottage with his parents, who are stern but understanding.

"I'd better gather up all these wrappers before mom and dad wake up to my Monday through Friday morning revelry," thought Lars. The lashing of a philosophical pep talk would be their first attack if they caught him red-handed. "The torture of the health talk about my increasing weight gain and the considerably unhealthy position I'm putting myself in, without direction or control, and so forth… Oh, how it would go on and on." Lars scooped up the evidence of his almost criminal act. His parents would persecute him as if he had truly committed a crime.

Lars dashed from his room keeping an eye on the doorknob that led to his parents' room, adjacent to his, tiptoeing as quiet as a mouse down the dim hallway. The hardwood floors did nothing to aid the overstuffed Lars, each step sounding off with a creaking and a cracking in his efforts to dispose of the evidence. Evidence that could possibly put him on punishment of some sort, like no sweets for a week. He thought how horribly impossible that would make his life, as he moved faster toward the garbage cans that stood outside.

At this point Lars was heading at top speed for the door as the floor was still a-creaking and a-cracking, reaching unbearably loud decibels, it seemed to Lars. It was taking forever to exit the hallway as if it had transformed into a carnival sideshow attraction: 'WELCOME TO THE NEVER-ENDING HALLWAY.' Finally, he reached the garbage cans, but in his haste, he missed a wrapper. Dumping his evidence, he made sure that all the wrappers were stuffed towards the bottom of the garbage can. He closed the garbage can lid and simultaneously wiped his forehead free of perspiration that had gathered on him. If not for the cool damp morning air, Lars might have shed a couple pounds from sweating.

Returning to the house, he noticed the yard was in a shambles, weeds growing everywhere; this was one of his assigned chores. In this case his parents had been lenient. It had been three months since the yard had been attended to. Lars held his head low as he slunk back into the house, complaining to himself, "It's going to take two days to clean up the yard. Why did I wait so long to do something about it? It's like I have no energy or drive to take care of my responsibilities. Again, I feel like I'm suffering from lack of self-esteem and willpower."

Just as he reached the infamous hallway, he spied, staring at him, a Sophie Soft Cupcake wrapper. It stood out from the furniture decorating the hallway. Startled, Lars panicked. He saw the doorknob slowly turning. He had to think fast, as it was his father leaving for work.

With briefcase in hand and an overcoat draped over his shoulder, an average height man and one who looked fit but could never fool a flight of stairs, his father acknowledged to his dear wife that he would be home for dinner tonight.

Mrs. Pushkin is a loving housewife and mother. Her accordion-shaped middle-aged body screams, 'Stop calling the kettle black.' She has also abandoned the habit of exercising. "That's fine, dear," she replies.

Quickly, Lars jumped to step on the wrapper that he had missed in the hallway. The resultant thud from Lars' leap alarmed Mr. Pushkin. He turned and faced Lars.

"Good morning, Dad," said Lars.

"Morning, son. You're up pretty early, what are you up to?"

"Just emptying the garbage." Using his craftiness, he kept the wrapper covered with his foot while making his way back to his room.

"What has gotten into you?" grinned Mr. Pushkin. "Time after time I've pulled my hair out trying to convince you of the importance of completing your responsibilities. This is a sign that it's going to be a great day," shouted Mr. Pushkin. Dancing down the hallway towards the kitchen, he wished Lars a wonderful day as he left for work.

Lars, with a sigh of relief, stated, "Whew—that was pretty close" Furtively he disposed of the last of the evidence of his morning gluttony.

Making his way to his room to get dressed for school, Lars' face displayed the flat and unsmiling eyes of a Gila monster. His lips and cheeks were drained of color. "It could have been curtains for me if I had been caught eating before breakfast," grinned Lars.

Lars, unlike some kids, had a difficult time bending over to tie his shoes. While sitting down, he had to literally take a deep breath to grab his shoelaces.

He belted out, "That's it, I'm fed up with this extra weight. Heck, I almost passed out from tying my shoes. I don't care what my belly starts craving, I'll decide whether it's time to eat and what to eat. I'm 12 years old in the sixth grade. I'm practically a man so it's time to make a man's decision. I'm going to put myself on a strict diet, start a ritual of exercising, walking and sit-ups, whatever I need to do."

As Lars was feeling around his midsection, the mirror conveyed the extent of his battle. "I will deal with this as war, I will triumph. I will bash my cravings with the thought of transformation. This body will soon be a body to die for. Muscular and toned from head to toes. Yeah," he belted. "They'll say, 'Wow, look at Lars. Look at Lars!'"

# Chapter 2

# Breakfast Battle

Just then, his confidence bubble collapsed from his mother's voice. "Breakfast is ready," she shouted. "Come and get it." Lars stood in front of the mirror with his hands still around his midsection. "This will be my first battle." Lars now felt full of confidence that he could walk right by his mother's famous breakfast.

With books and hoodie in hand he proceeded towards the kitchen on his way to leaving for school. At the kitchen doorway, Lars was halted by the beckoning aromas that began to invade all his senses.

Mrs. Pushkin checked off the morning breakfast like a used-car salesman on grand opening day. "Pancakes, biscuits, omelets, fried potatoes, bacon, sausage, milk or juice." Lars' eyes widened inch by inch after hearing each item. His stomach started to growl as it struggled to make room due to all those cupcakes he had chowed down on earlier. "I must stick to my new resolutions; I just can't give in." Lars looked like he had this battle licked.

Lo and behold, Mr. 'T' appeared. Lars' strength began to dwindle, dwindle down to where he finally submitted to Mr. 'T'.

"Lars, the energy you're going to need must be fueled with your mom's breakfast. She took all that time to cook for you. Your mom doesn't have a clue about the cupcakes. For all she knows this is your first meal," Mr. 'T' snickered.

"So, go on and eat those delicious hot buttered pancakes drowned in maple syrup, and don't forget the extras."

That's what Mr. 'T' keeps hidden in his trench coat: negative suggestions for bad eating. Mr. 'T's suggestions won over Lars until he gave in. He lost this battle. Lars delightedly pulled his fork away from his lips as if each bite contained zero calories. His mind was telling him he wouldn't gain any weight. He chugged down the last of his milk, acquiring a milk mustache.

He pushed himself from the table, simultaneously giving off an extra-large belch, politely responding, "Excuse me."

"Thanks, Mom, for breakfast," exclaimed Lars, while waddling out the door for school, now quite upset with himself for allowing Mr. 'T' to convince him to pig out at breakfast knowing he had devoured a dozen cupcakes earlier on.

•

# Chapter 3

# Lars Schemes With Shellmond

Overstuffed, he began his walk to school. He was Most uncomfortable; it was more of a waddle then a walk. "Oh boy, my stomach feels like a giant watermelon ready to cut and serve. Consequences, is what I'm suffering from, this is exactly what I deserve. A battle lost— but the war is not over. I will persevere."

He began breathing heavily as he reached each corner. Lars built up a sweat. His jeans seem to fit tighter than usual.

He met his friend, Shellmond, at the intersection. His close friend, Shellmond also carried extra luggage around his midsection.

"Hey, Lars."

"Hi, Shellmond," replied Lars with a crooked smile as if he had been struck with a sudden gas pain.

"Did Mr. 'T' visit you this morning again?" Shellmond asked, as Lars tugged at his belt to loosen it. The unpleasant thought changed Lars' expression to the signal of defeat. "Yeah, he did. I really felt like I could have overcome Mr. 'T'."

Lars continued, "The giant cupcake sale they had yesterday at the market proved to be a little overwhelming for me. Mom and I were shopping for groceries and then, wham, there they were, mouthwatering, deliciously displayed cupcakes. Every kind you can think of staring at me."

Shellmond, in awe of the variety of cupcakes Lars described, felt a shimmer of slobber on his lip. He wiped his lips and replied, "Your mother bought you cupcakes?"

Lars replied, "Of course not. I devised a plan to be able to purchase some of those delicious- looking cupcakes myself."

Pacing themselves to reach the school building, it came into view just a few blocks ahead.

"What did you come up with to acquire those delicious-sounding cupcakes?"

Puffing and panting from the walk, Lars replied, "Well, while mom and I were loading up the car with our groceries, I noticed several elderly shoppers who could use some help with loading their groceries in their carts and cars. Immediately, I began seeking out those who wanted help. I told my mom I would walk home from here when I was done helping.

"Well, my mom thought it was a grand idea and considerate of me, not knowing the true purpose of my crusade. She hugged me, grabbing my backpack, saying, 'Let me lighten your load,' not knowing I might have to use my backpack for containing cupcakes, which I couldn't let her know. Thanks, Mom."

"I began to hustle and bustle all through the parking lot of the market helping those who needed it, asking everyone who seemed to require my services. I must admit, I felt a sparkle inside when the faces of the elderly lit up in sheer delight when I offered to assist them. To make a long story short, I was able to purchase a dozen cupcakes, each individually distinctive. Now the hard part."

Shellmond interrupted, "Yeah, I'm waiting to hear how you cleverly snuck a dozen cupcakes into your room."

"At first I thought I had it all figured out. I'd simply do one of my afternoon chores, which is to empty the waste baskets in the house. The first waste basket would naturally be mine. I could leave the cupcakes outside by the outdoor trashcans, retrieve the trashcan from my room, empty it and fill it with my cupcakes, then come back in casually. Bingo, I would have a dozen, mouth-watering cupcakes at my disposal, and I started to do just that."

"As planned, I left the bag of cupcakes beside the garbage can outside." Lars smiled that boyish grin, a hearty contagious smile, a smile that promoted false confidence. As he had carefully put together his plan, he felt he couldn't fail.

His mom greeted him at the door. "Hello, Lars." He quickly answered, "Hi." His voice dissipated as he made his way towards his room at a hurried pace.

"How was your day?" shouted Lars. She began to tell him. In different rooms her voice sounded far off in the distance. Lars made his way to his waste basket. He was shocked and almost appalled to find it empty. Now Lars dashed to the bathroom. Empty waste baskets were what he found. He made a fast break for his parents' room. No luck there, his chore of emptying the waste baskets was done.

Meanwhile, Mrs. Pushkin's conversation about her day continued. Then Lars faintly overheard that his dad was given a promotion, which called for a celebration.

Mrs. Pushkin boasted, "I was overjoyed, so I cleaned all the rooms today and cooked a special meal." Lars was stunned. Shellmond was silent, his face showing dismay.

Lars didn't lose hope. He carefully went from room to room, looking for ways to get those cupcakes in undetected. As he was just about to run out of ideas Lars was hit with a foolproof plan upon glancing at the vacuum cleaner.

"Looks like the vacuum bag needs to be emptied," shouted Lars. Mrs. Pushkin replied, "Thank you, Lars that's one thing I did forget to do."

Shellmond interrupted, "Why Lars, you're a genius. You put the cupcakes in the vacuum after emptying it."

"Correct," exclaimed Lars. "Such a genius that I've engineered a very uncomfortable stomachache."

As they were crossing the last intersection before reaching the schoolyard, Lars revealed to his friend, "I also ate breakfast." As he made this comment, he simultaneously passed a large cloud of gas.

Shellmond sidestepped quickly in order not to get a whiff of Lars' flatulence. "You mean your mom's famous breakfast?" Shellmond inched farther away, saying, "Wow!" as the smell of decayed pancakes and cupcakes permeated the air.

# Chapter 4

# Schoolyard Struggles

An overcast day that joined forces with a brisk breeze helped clear the air as Lars and Shellmond approached the schoolyard.

The schoolyard was packed. Kickball games here, basketball games there. Two long lines of kids patiently waiting to race each other. There were kids waiting to play tetherball. The game of tag was in effect with many players, which sometimes interfered with the other games in progress. Nevertheless, it was a scene of chaotic fun.

Lars looked on with remorse, knowing his condition would hinder him in competing in the early morning schoolyard activities. Lars looks at Shellmond. "I also failed to mention I have set a goal. I'm at war with Mr. 'T'. I'm going to fight Mr. 'T' with everything I've got. ARE YOU WITH ME?"

Shellmond just grew a centimeter of pure confidence. "Lars, I'm in, let's do this. This really could work for us. As a team we can really keep each other on the straight and narrow."

Lars exclaimed, "When one of us is weakening the other will step up and give that helping pep talk, build that resistance against temptation, better known as Mr. 'T'."

Lars continued, "Man, I really feel good about this. I'm feeling my resistance strengthening at this very moment. I'm gonna put a hurtin' on Mr. 'T'. What the heck, let's jump into that game of tag."

Shellmond cringed at the idea. "But Lars, they're running all over the school yard.

You think you can keep up with that? Look at them running through the kickball games. Those long lines of patient kids waiting to race each other? They are disturbing the basketball games; we are not in that kind of shape."

Lars said, "Ha, you wait here. Watch me tag somebody in." Shellmond looked on, witnessing the verbal badgering of Lars by the other kids. Lars' ears were burning with the heckling: "Fat boy can't run, he can't tag anybody."

Pouring out energy like never before, trying to keep up with the others, they dodged in and out of congested areas on the yard. Where Lars' size would create a problem getting through, he would use an alternate route. This placed him amid the ongoing schoolyard games.

The badgering elevated. "Dang, Lars you're in the way."

"Move, fat boy."

"Watch out, Lars."

Then, as if things couldn't get any worse, Lars heard, "Look out!"

Bop, the kickball slapped Lars on the forehead. Lars saw stars and began to fall back. His good old buddy, Shellmond, caught him in an instant.

The morning bell sounded off. Everyone froze until the bell stopped, followed by the routine of classmates forming a line with their teachers to enter their classrooms.

The students chuckled, pointed fingers and whispered about Lars' school yard participation. Shellmond boasted, "I'll give you an A for effort, an F for timing.

This isn't the right time, Lars."

Shellmond helped Lars to the classroom line. "Yeah, you're right, I really captured attention in the wrong way." They both displayed tickled grins.

# Chapter 5

# Quiz Quandary

"School now is in session, paper and pencils out," ordered Ms. Dunne.

"We are having a quick quiz and then we have an assembly in the auditorium.

We have a special guest."

"Quiz, oh boy," murmured Lars. Taking tests was not one of Lars' best attributes.

On the other hand, Shellmond loved tests and quizzes.

"Remember, we're in this together, Shellmond old pal. Whenever one of us needs help, the other is there for total support," smirked Lars.

Their classmates had empathy for Lars and Shellmond. Since they're the roundest in the school, they don't give them a bad time. It's the kids from room 206 that could really get under their skins. Room 205, Lars' class, has the best kickball players, the fastest runners and the best-looking teacher. They also have the roundest kids in the school, Lars and Shellmond. They are the targets of every jealous kid who's not in room 205.

Shellmond was engaged vigorously in the quiz while Lars struggled. He tried to view Shellmond's answers. Shellmond saw his efforts and tried to assist him by scooting the answers toward the edge of his desk. Simultaneously, Lars tried to slide his desk in order to get a better view. He began to lean over and fell sideways onto the floor.

"BOOM!" Down went Lars. His classmates went into an uproar. Kids were laughing themselves out of their seats. Shellmond couldn't restrain his laughter for a moment; then quickly he gathered himself to support his friend. Laughter filled the room. Lars scanned the obvious amusement on the faces of his classmates except one, a girl.

Lars was now entering a new territory—girls. At twelve years of age, he was acquiring hormones which he knew nothing about, but he had noticed something. "Tina's not laughing about you," observed Shellmond. "She even looks like…yep, she's coming over here," he whispered.

"Hi, Lars, are you all right?" Tina asked, as Lars brushed himself off from the incriminating fall.

"Yeah, I'm fine, thanks, Tina."

"Everybody got a good laugh about it but you, why?" asked Lars.

"Well, I saw what happened in the school yard and now this quiz. I said to myself that person could use a friend right about now."

"I felt a little embarrassed, just a little," said Lars, "just a little."

"Well, Lars, everyone has those days when nothing seems to go right no matter how hard you try. My parents taught me that it can't always be bad and it can't always be good, there is a balance in life. No one is perfect. I listen to my parents and try to act according to their guidance."

"Wow, all that confidence coming from this frail, redheaded, pale-skinned girl who stands taller than I. She sounds so sure of herself. I want that for myself," Lars thought. "Tina, you're all right for a girl."

"Attention, attention," shrieked Ms. Dunne. "Back to your seats and finish the quiz. Lars, are you okay?"

"Yes, I'm okay," Lars answered.

"Good, now how about finishing that quiz?" Ms. Dunne is an attractive woman with a figure that belongs in a Ferrari. All the male teachers are awestruck when she's present among them. "You have five minutes left, then we're off to the assembly."

Lars saw that the quiz really wasn't as hard as he had made it out to be.

Buckling down with determination to beat the clock to complete the quiz, his focus was prominent as the curl of his mouth helped him retrieve the answers.

Daydreaming momentarily set in. Lars was captivated by the hardwood parquet floor, stained wooden-framed doorway, and the Gothic-looking light fixtures, accompanied by wired windowpanes that made up room 205.

"Time's up, pass all quizzes up to the front," ordered Ms. Dunne.

# Chapter 6

# Auditorium Amazement

The sounds of pitter-patter echoed in the school hallways. Hundreds of pairs of shoes were screeching, scuffling, and shuffling to make way for the assembly. Pounding joyful hearts raced to the auditorium as if they were headed to the amusement park. The auditorium reached capacity. The door closed and the lights began to dim.

"Ooh!" and "Ahh!" reactions were heard as the auditorium darkened.

The principal of the school, Mr. Lynch approached the stage, greeting the students and faculty, "Good morning, everyone."

"Good morning Mr. Lynch," replied the standing room only assembly as a scrawny little man, whose greasy hair shone in the stage lights, took center stage.

"Today we have an incredibly special guest, a magician," said Mr. Lynch. The sea of bubbly faces looked on. "Before the introduction, we'll go through our daily calendar." They heard about the free lunch program, book drive and cupcake sales.

"Okay, kids— here's what we've all been waiting for! Introducing Mir, the Magician who will show us some special magic tricks."

"Tricks! Tricks!" blurted Mir the Magician, as he cleared his voice. "Here! here! My good man, I assure you they are not tricks. It's magic!" belted Mir.

The special guest, who decided to introduce himself to the standing room only auditorium, gracefully stepped in front of Mr. Lynch, while simultaneously pushing him aside.

"I'm called Mir the Magician, and I have performed all over the world. You name it, I've been there, showing my abilities to produce mind-boggling magic.

I didn't bring my entire show here for you, though, as your auditorium stage is a bit small for all my props."

Moans and sighs floated through the packed house.

"Nevertheless, what I have for you all today will amaze you, so let's begin."

Mir the Magician began his routine, with disappearing and appearing acts from birds to flying cards, to rabbits out of his hat, just to name a few.

The crowded auditorium was overwhelmed with curiosity. His magic unquestionably proved to be authentic, as he went on guessing people's names, ages, and places of birth. Blindfolded, he mesmerized everyone by trying to guess the number of people in the auditorium.

Mir the Magician faced a standing ovation as the show ended. He bowed and gave thanks to all the onlookers. At that instant the stage went dark, then the lights came up brightly. Mir the Magician had vanished.

The stage was completely empty, props and all. A confused Mr. Lynch approached the stage to dismiss the assembly, wondering, "Where did the magician go?"

# Chapter 7

# Benny the Bully

Unfortunately, Lars didn't get to really enjoy the show due to the bullies that plagued the school. This one particular kid Benny had it in for Lars. Lars didn't understand why. Lars tried his best to stay clear of Benny, but that didn't help.

Benny was a kid neanderthal of intimidating height. He continuously looked for Lars just to bully him. For instance, during the magic show Benny embarrassed Lars in different ways. Some kids found it funny, some kids didn't. Lars, of course, became upset and mad.

"It's kids' school law, you don't snitch when you get picked on. It looks bad, makes you look weak." Lars pondered this attitude, but found no solution.

Meanwhile the heckling increased until it was finally noticed by a teacher whom removed Benny from his auditorium seat to the Principal's office. As Benny was escorted out, he made mean eye contact with Lars, as if Lars had something to do with his removal.

Mr. Lynch asked if everyone could calmly return to their classes. Instead, the kids took that request as, "Start up your engines and let's see who can get back to class the fastest." Pure pandemonium ensued.

The distinctive sound of classroom doors closing filled the hallways.

Then silence: you could hear a pin drop. Instructions for the next lesson were to pair off with your reading partners. Reading chapters in

History could be boring unless your reading partner was Tina. Lars has Tina on the brain.

The empty desk next to Lars soon was filled with a reading partner. He was stunned. Multiple questions crossed his mind. "Tina sat next to me, why?"

Students scampered through the room like socks in a washer to pair up.

The two locked eyes and conversed in a stare. In his mind Lars is saying, "Say something! This staring is not going to last, even though it's a pleasant stare."

Meanwhile, Tina was wondering, "Is Lars going to say anything?"

Lars chuckled, smiled his boyish contagious grin and said, "Hey, Tina, I was going to ask you to pair up with me for reading, what a coincidence."

Lars noticed he was slightly sweating as he worked to advance the conversation.

Tina replied, "Certainly," as the two sat together. Enjoying reading and listening to alternating paragraphs, they slipped in their own personal conversations about school, faculty, school policies and most of all, bullies.

All that anxiety that had been spawned that day held no existence during those few exclusive moments with Tina.

The last bell of the day sounded off. As the school emptied out, Lars and Shellmond made a mad dash for a route they had mapped out to avoid being bullied. In no time they were clear of any danger. The boys separated.

Shellmond headed home for his after-school chores, while Lars went on his trek to the supermarket.

# Chapter 8

# Supermarket Surprise

Planning on creating a job, possibly a helper who assists customers with their groceries from the store to their vehicles, the manager of Biggs Grocery Store had reservations at first, as the possibility of liability came to mind. Knowing Lars to be a respectable kid, he allowed him to assist the store's patrons in the parking lot after signing a liability disclosure.

Lars' first day at work was exhausting. The afternoon overcast sky partnered Lars, giving him a cool environment to work in. He helped elderly couples, seniors that were handicapped, pregnant mothers shopping solo, just anyone who needed help. They all saw Lars' enthusiasm radiating so brightly. Lars' face shone with pride.

Finished for the day, Lars retrieved his backpack and school hoodie that all students were required to wear. As he left the employees' locker room, there might have been one or two employees who acknowledged him as a coworker.

"Good night Lars, see you tomorrow."

Heading home, Lars veered off to a main artery of the town to reach his destination. Lo and behold, his nemesis the neanderthal bully, Benny, happened to be walking towards him.

"This is not going to be good." Lars contemplated.

Benny began his routine of word bashing, to belittle Lars. Accepting cruel verbal lashings, Lars stood strong, showing no emotions. But inside the abuse was leaving an inevitable sense of sadness. Benny felt like he wasn't getting anywhere. His anger grew toward Lars, and he made an attempt to swing at Lars. The swing was caught in midair. Surprisingly, it was Mir the Magician, who had appeared out of nowhere.

"Dear boy, we will not have any of that, why, I can't have you injuring my apprentice," chided Mir. "There's a lot of work to be done so I need him healthy and injury-free. You run along now." Mir released Benny's arm, which he had held behind Benny's back. Benny took off running.

"I don't know what to say but thank you. Mir, where were you? How could you just appear like that?"

He chuckled, "I'm a magician, not only a magician, I'm Mir the Magician." They embraced with laughter.

Truly excited, Lars asked Mir, "When do we start my apprenticeship?"

"No, no, son. I just used that as our story for Benny. To be my apprentice you'd have to leave everything you know and love, and begin vigorous training. Your path leads elsewhere for you to find. But I'll be around for a while—I like this town. It's getting late. You'd better get home."

Lars agreed and scampered off, waving to Mir.

"Hope to see you again," exclaimed Lars.

# Chapter 9

# Dinnertime Dilemma

Minutes away, almost home, Lars' mind was invaded by the annoying Mr. 'T'.

Mr. 'T' screamed out, "IT'S TIME, LARS!" while teasing his taste buds with thoughts of Sophie Soft cupcakes. Sophie also baked an assortment of other desserts, with which Mr. 'T" tormented Lars.

"You've done well on tips today at work, so treat yourself."

Lars felt hopeless, so close to home, but he had to resist. "Just get inside the house and you'll be safe," he told himself.

The persistent Mr. 'T', short for Mr. Temptation, taunted Lars, "You don't want to go home without your goodies, do you?" he whispered with a sinister snicker. Lars was torn, and frightened. Despite every inch of his willpower battling Mr. 'T', Lars succumbed. Detouring, he stopped in at a nearby convenience store to purchase some Sophie Soft calories.

Approaching the walkway to his home he devoured the last of the delights.

Lars' remaining willpower was whisked away, with the aroma of pecan cake, his favorite.

Mr. 'T', with a sinister giggle, stated, "Sure hope you have room for that. Mother will know something's up if you don't bite down on your favorite cake."

Phasing Mr. 'T' out, Lars concluded "Between Benny and Mr. 'T', I'm going to need real help. That's it, I'll tell Mir the Magician my situation to see if he can help me find a solution."

Lars greeted his mother at the kitchen entrance. "I baked your favorite cake," Mrs. Pushkin revealed. With a generic grin and a bloated tummy, Lars answered, "Thank you very much, Mom."

"Your father will be late again, so it will just be us having dinner," she added.

"Okay," shouted Lars as he ran upstairs to change his school clothes into something more comfortable. The two had dinner and talked over their daily activities. Lars talked about his day and his mom did the same. Of course, Lars didn't mention anything about Benny the bully, or Mir the Magician, just Tina, his new friend. The in-depth discussion between Lars and his mom made the cleaning of the kitchen go quickly to end the evening.

# Chapter 10

# Morning Meal Misfire

Streaking sunrays passing through the window blinds awakened Lars for a new day. Like clockwork the inescapable breakfast was brewing. The scent of Mrs. Pushkin's breakfast could be used as a welcoming alarm, giving Lars a 'burst out of bed and race to the kitchen table' effect. Lars didn't need any assistance to race to the kitchen table. He had Mr. 'T' to alert him when it was time to fill his stomach—and Mr. 'T' appeared, right on cue.

"Lars," Mr. 'T' whispered. "You know what's cooking in the kitchen, let's show Mom our appreciation and fill that stomach." Answering back, Lars retorted, "I'm not going to fill my stomach to where it repays me with uncomfortable bloating and unnecessary gas. Not going to do it, my plate will be moderate or less." Lars thought, "I'm still at war with Mr. 'T', but so far, the battles have been in his favor."

Lars took his time preparing himself for school, with a morning hygiene cleanse, fresh underclothes, then his school uniform, including his hoodie.

Lars slid his seat up for the morning buffet. Mrs. Pushkin always cooked for a family of ten where there were only three. You name it, it was on the table.

Meanwhile Mr. Pushkin was already grooming himself to look presentable for today's meeting, nurturing an appetite as well.

His parents greeted Lars at the table, captivated. All three of them began to eat and eat. Mr. Pushkin was the first to give in. "No more, I'm full to the hilt."

Lars replied, "Not I." His creed of moderation or less had failed again, thanks to Mr. 'T', who seemed to have won another battle in this war.

Lars rinsed his palate with a glass of milk and wiped his mouth. He then realized, "Bam! Darn it, I did it again." His stomach felt like a water-filled fish tank being moved from one place to another. Departing the kitchen, Lars thanked his mother for breakfast and wished both his parents a wonderful day.

# Chapter 11

# Schoolyard Situation

Off to school Lars went; he couldn't ask for a prettier day. Cloudless skies joined the sun's rays to dance all over, providing Vitamin D for everyone. As Lars and Shellmond approached their intersection, they greeted each other with a mass of dialog that took them all the way to school.

Upon entering the main hall, Lars spotted the neanderthal kid Benny, leaning against the lockers. In a panic, wanting to be unnoticed, Lars tried to scamper past him. Benny stopped Lars in his tracks and started to taunt Lars, as usual, once more bullying him in the hallway. A faculty member gave a concerned look at the two. He interrupted the verbal lashing and shoving. In an instant Benny was escorted to the Dean's office.

"Saved again," thought Lars, with a sigh of thankfulness.

"Oh, you again," said the Dean, Mr. Jung, to Benny. He was a wiry, middle-aged man, of medium height, with strong convictions. "Benny, you know the drill. Take that seat in the middle of the floor. You sit in it until I say otherwise."

Benny is known well at the Dean's office. He basically has a permanent desk there, which is placed in the middle of the room. He's well-known for picking fights with the weaker and overweight students; going so far as to snatch other students' lunches and snacks. Unfortunately, he's just had a bad start in life; with a little direction and foundation, he'll straighten up. But until then?

A sympathetic Shellmond grabbed Lars by the arm and rushed him to the schoolyard. "Come on Lars, let's see what we can get into. A game or something before homeroom bell rings." Lars and Shellmond scanned the yard, surfaced in rubber asphalt that reached from end to end. A sea of kids paired off into different activities.

Lars and Shellmond decided to play kickball. They were picked to play and were on opposite teams, thanks to the absence of Benny. Benny's followers were okay long as Benny was not around. Lars' team was up. The kicking orders had Lars kicking fourth, what they call 'cleanup'.

The first kicker reached first base. So did the second as well as the third, then Lars came up. Nervous as a patient first visiting the dentist, and looking not to blunder again, he concentrated on the pitch obsessively.

He thought, "If I can kick the ball into the outfield, I can bring my teammates in to score. On the other hand, I can try to kick with all my might and miss. That'll bring laughter to the schoolyard." Lars found himself facing a dilemma.

Lars waited on the pitch, and just as it was released the homeroom bell rang.

All schoolyard activities ceased. Relief was the best description for Lars' emotions, knowing he could have had another mishap on the schoolyard blacktop.

# Chapter 12

# Mir the Magician's Method

"Who would like to read today's bulletin?" exclaims Ms. Dunne. There was a moment of voluntary silence. "Hmm, all right then; I'll pick. Shellmond, a shy respectable boy, lacking in confidence, walked to the front of the class and began reading today's bulletin. He read off the problems on campus: theft, fighting, bullying, keeping the schoolyard, hallways and cafeteria clean.

Graciously, some schoolteachers had decided to add a little flair to Delwood Middle School's activities. Their plan was to put on an art class and contest, which would be judged at the end of the month. The classes would be held during lunch time. Lunches are acceptable during the art class.

"I'll sign up for that." Lars announced. "I'll be out of harm's way during lunch, avoiding Benny."

After some discussion of the bulletin, the morning's lesson commenced.

In class Lars overheard a complaint by a classmate, stipulating how his lunch was taken yesterday by Benny, and that he wasn't the only one that day. The student dared not tell an administrator. The outcome could be bad for that person—a retaliation would be in order from Benny. Hearing this, Lars discovered that he wasn't the only one on Benny's hit list. Benny was certainly making life miserable for some of the students at Delwood. Surely there must be a way to get even.

"Lunchtime is near," Ms. Dunne conveyed. "You can put away your lessons now."

In the midst of preparing for lunch, Lars asked to go to the lavatory. Permission was granted. As he exited the lavatory, the door accidentally hit a student who was coming in. That student just happened to be Benny.

"Why, you fat dummy, watch where you're going," snarled Benny, producing a cold stare.

At that point, Lars felt isolated and vulnerable. "Excuse me, I'm sorry," he murmured, which wasn't enough as Benny shoved Lars firmly.

"Move, get out of my way," said Benny, showing his aggressive bitterness.

Lars did just that—with a cringing smile he got out of Benny's way in a hurry. He realized it could have been worse. "It was just us two alone in the hallway," he muttered, shaking.

As Lars headed back to class before the lunch bell, out of nowhere materialized Mir the Magician, seemingly an angel for Lars, always there at the right time.

"I have something for you. I understand that Benny has a problem of taking other students' lunches, snacks and money if they have it. Well, here's some candy that I want you to pass around to those who are having issues with Benny. Instruct them not to consume it themselves, even though it looks like chocolate candy. In reality, it's a laxative—a harmless way of teaching Benny a lesson, the lesson that one should not take things from another. This is our secret—and you haven't seen me," Mir said, as Lars turned to go down the hall.

The lunchtime bell chimed. Lars viewed the clock in the hallway; it read 12:00. Worried that Mir would be seen by the traffic jam of students rushing for lunch, Lars peered back over his shoulder. The magician had simply vanished.

During lunch Lars passed out the laxatives disguised as candies to the victims of choice that Benny most loved to taunt. Lars told them the instructions, telling them not to eat these chocolate bits, and the reason why.

"Today is the art class signup," the art instructor states. "Those who want to participate, please form a line." Waiting to sign up, the group of students were excited and eager, looking forward to drawing on canvas.

Little did Lars know, Tina was interested in the art class, too. With no hesitation he waved Tina over.

"You can get in front of me," he gestured to her. Others looked on with a frown, but nothing was said. Tina gave a gratifying reply, "Thanks Lars, you really are a cool guy."

They talked and joked like old friends while waiting to sign up, producing a genuine bond of friendship. Friendship, not relationship, which Lars has known little of in his life. "She could possibly see me as a person of interest," he pondered.

Lars felt truly blessed to have one of Delwood Middle School's attractive females as a good friend. He thought, "If people see us interacting, I must be a pretty good guy. That's how you acquire friends," reflected Lars.

After signing up for the lunchtime art class and contest talk, Lars was travelling the schoolyard. Benny was at it again, strong-arming students for their goodies.

Lars met up with Shellmond. "Hey, Lars, what's up? Where have you been?"

"Tina and I have decided to enter the art class contest."

"So did I," gloated Shellmond. "You must have been first in line; I didn't see you. You and Tina, no way."

"Well, to be honest, I happened to be in the line when we saw each other. I waved her over to go before me."

"Are you trying to pursue Tina?"

"No." replied Lars. "We have established a solid friendship and nothing more."

"Wow, how lucky can you get to have a friend so pretty?" exclaimed Shellmond.

"Blessed is the best word to describe that," Lars replied.

"Listen, there's a few things I haven't mentioned to you yet. It's about Mir the Magician and our buddy Benny."

"Buddy, ha! He's no buddy of ours."

Shellmond got an earful on what happened to Lars that day and the day before.

"Now we wait patiently for some chocolate candy results." By this time, a couple other students who had had a run-in with Benny joined the boys on the bench.

# Chapter 13

## Benny Hits Bottom

On that particular bench sat Benny's victims, and those victims had their chocolate candy taken. All eyes were on Benny, who was playing basketball. As usual, he exploited his character, being obnoxious and playing unfairly, causing the game to run in disarray.

Finally, Benny's victims saw evidence the chocolate candy was taking effect.

Benny went up for a shot with the ball and came down holding his stomach and butt. He made a mad dash to the bathroom. The bench became a scene of unstoppable laughter for they knew Benny's dilemma. Other students who were around didn't know what all the laughter was about. They were told,

"He who laughs last is slow." They joined in anyway, and soon the whole schoolyard was in an uproar.

The lunch break bell rerouted the kids back to class.

Using a similar lesson plan to the day before, spacing the desks, Ms. Dunne ordered Lars and Shellmond to sit apart for the day's quiz.

The end of the school day arrived. Students dispersed to attend to their after-school interests or chores, and Lars went on his way to Biggs Grocery Store. Whispers were filling the hallways, stating that Benny didn't make it to the bathroom—and it was gross. These whispers were pleasing to Lars, providing a sense of vindication, and he danced all the way to work.

Biggs Grocery Store happened to be very busy today. Lars was in double-time mode. He was stretched, covering the entire parking lot. No doubt he may have shaved off a couple of inches. As Lars was building up a good sweat, a thoughtful co-worker brought Lars a bottle of water. "You look dehydrated," the co-worker said.

Guzzling down the water as if he was walking the Sahara Desert, Lars contemplated the authentic bonding of Benny's victims. They all made a pact to keep what happened a secret.

The three hours of work flew by as the workday came to a close for Lars. Like clockwork, Mr. 'T' made his presence known.

"You did well for yourself, Lars. Don't you think it's time for a little gratuity?" Lars fought hard, waging war with Mr. 'T'. It didn't last long, but Lars made an admirable attempt. Lars went home with six Sophie Soft Cupcakes.

The next day Lars woke up annoyed at having lost another battle with Mr. 'T'. "This war I am fighting will go on until I win," said Lars to himself, speaking firmly.

"I always sound so confident after the fact."

Devouring Mrs. Pushkin's over-indulgent breakfast, Lars saluted his Mom with a delightful grin.

"Have a wonderful day, Mom."

# Chapter 14

# Beware of Benny

Bright and vivid sunlight painted the scene, selective rays descended, warming Lars on his trek to school. Delwood Middle School sat in the heart of a quaint hospitable neighborhood in his town. The blue sky gave the green light to a flight of migratory birds flapping towards the horizon. It was a desirable place for its inhabitants.

Beyond all this bliss, of course, one could find neighborhoods composed of a hundred cinder-block clones, decorated with broken-bicycle-cluttered front yards. One of those was Benny's neighborhood.

On other streets were the two-story homes of prosperous families, trimmed with scrolled-iron balconies, and featuring custom black iron gates.

The neighborhood homes were either identical twins or possessed their own identity. Little if any traffic drove down these streets. Cars seemed to pause and purr with curious satisfaction. The little town rested on a few slightly graded hills. Lars couldn't ask for an easier route to school.

Once he met Shellmond at their designated intersection, they took turns rambling.

They talked about Benny's dilemma and what action he was going to take.

They speculated about the first day of art class, and how it would bring them sure delight. They also discussed Shellmond's getting a bagger job like Lars. They talked about battling Mr. 'T'. Their intense conversation took them all the way to school.

Entering the schoolyard, the boys joined up with the few students who had suffered Benny's meanness. They waited with bated breath to witness a different demeanor from Benny. They hoped to see maybe a little humbleness, kindness—after all, he had to be embarrassed. No one in their right mind would mention his accident. It was not a good idea to stir Benny up, as he was pretty ruthless.

Benny arrived at school. He showed an unwholesome lack of emotion, as if he were a wick for someone to light, so he could explode.

Still suffering from the shock of success, the group of boys made eye contact with Benny. Strait-laced; nothing out of order, their facial expressions stayed neutral. No one wanted to give away that they knew of his unfortunate accident.

His demeanor dictated trouble.

A basketball game was going on, and both teams were evenly matched. The onlookers were entertained by the playing of both squads in a very exciting game.

To the dismay of everyone, Benny made a nuisance of himself, jumping into the middle of the game, and took the ball away to shoot by himself.

Half the schoolyard yelled out to him, "Give the ball back so they can finish the game." Benny acted purposely to agitate his victims, to intimidate someone who would speak out about his messy mishap. But no one did. They kept their composure.

The first bell rang for class time. Benny's attitude to life might have something to do with his unhealthy background. He spent most of his childhood years in turmoil; passing through the revolving doors of several foster homes was a start.

Benny was from a family of six siblings, who were all separated at an early age. His home town was ravaged by extremes of weather at all seasons. Finally, his present foster parents decided to move. In this new town, his foster parents thought he could get a new start, make friends and try to finish school without getting expelled.

In his old town, he had problems getting along with students at school. He was actually the hunted, with no intervention from anyone. He began to act accordingly. He found out carrying an angry attitude kept he bullies away.

As the years went on, Benny grew faster than most kids his age. Eventually, those who once were bullies were no more. Benny had certainly put fear in them.

Other downsides of Benny's troubles were stealing and vandalism. Apprehended and charged, he did a fourteen-month stint at a camp for first-time offenders. He became a prime candidate for serial delinquency.

## Chapter 15

# Lars' Friends and Their Family Facts

In room 205 a few students chattered during reading. They were stunned by Benny's disrupting the most exciting game in months. The talk was about who was going to stand up to Benny. He really needed a stronger message.

The conversation went on and on; no one was doing any reading. Ms. Dunne corrected all that with a stern suggestion. "If you have read those 15 paragraphs completely, we can start the quiz now."

"Noooo!" screamed the students. Soon silence fell, as everyone became engulfed in today's reading.

Tina, who was Lars' reading partner, finished her paragraphs and began the quiz. Meanwhile, Lars had a few paragraphs left. His brain was stifled by daydreaming. Half his mind was on reading; the other half on Tina. "How smart she is," he thought, not knowing yet that her parents are professors at the nearby college.

Tina comes from a studious family. Two older sisters groomed her from the time she was an infant. As a native of the quaint wholesome little town, she is destined to be successful. Her family thrives on harmony and equality.

Any source of negativity that invades their home evaporates quickly. Everyone pitches in to do their share of responsibilities. It cements their family values and approach to life.

Lars finally completed the fifteen paragraphs and started the quiz. Coincidentally, Shellmond was reaching for a quiz sheet at the same time.

Shellmond also comes from a family that shares each other's joy and happiness. With a family of twelve, there was no room for nonsense. Shellmond, being the middle child of the clan, had an incredible upbringing from his older siblings. He was taught the necessities. To get along in life, he had to respect his elders, respect his parents, avoid things that could create trouble and treat all people as he would like to be treated.

In contrast to Lars' mother's well-kept home, Shellmond's home was a 24-hour diner. It baffled Lars how Shellmond's mother could keep food on the table for twelve, at all times. What an amazing feat!

Shellmond was also at war with Mr. 'T'. It was a losing battle for him; so far, he faced the same outcome as Lars. What he had been taught about life, he passed down to his younger siblings. He encouraged them not to let their guards down, and to fight for what they felt was right, especially about overeating.

"Don't take the road I took," he advised them. "Being overweight hinders you in everything you do. Nip it in the bud."

The students were finishing their quizzes. Shellmond passed his paper in. He slid Lars a note. "It's time for me to join you on a quest to fight Mr. 'T'.

Shellmond was ready to beat that feeling that he needed something sweet; to beat the snacking between meals, and, most of all work on losing plenty of inches.

Ms. Dunne abruptly stopped the quiz. "Time is up, put your folders away. The bell is about to ring for lunch," she barked.

Off they went to the cafeteria. Lars planned to grab a free lunch that was offered and head to the first day of art class. As the free lunches were issued out, there was a disturbance in line.

"I'm getting really ill about that Benny. Why can't he wait in line like the rest of us?" Lars thought. Benny had cut in front of some students to receive a free lunch. The kid that stood up to Benny showed spunk and courage, but still Benny stayed in line to receive the free lunch first.

"I observed something in Benny that showed me he's not so tough. Someone someday will change Benny's character," Lars thought.

## Chapter 16

# Mir's Major Message

Lars sprinted to art class after grabbing his free lunch from the cafeteria, as fast as he could run, which unfortunately was equivalent to running in sand. As Lars took a short cut, a stairwell seldom used, Mir the Magician happened to appear. They greeted each other.

"Hey, Mir, what you are doing here?" asked Lars, startled.

"I've been watching, and I've decided to help you get over your small obstacles in life that are confining you. Here I hold a special heirloom that's been in my family for generations. It possesses certain powers that can build courage, focus, discipline and instincts. It basically everything you're made of," explained Mir. "Keep this heirloom in your hoodie coin pocket that's sewn on underneath the zipper." This was a pocket Lars never knew existed.

"The heirloom is the size of a quarter. Here are the rules to follow. If you don't, the heirloom won't produce for you. First, once I place it in your coin pocket you can never remove it to show anyone. You can never view it yourself. Always keep the heirloom in that pocket. I'll ask for it back later."

Lars replied in an astonished voice, "I don't know what to say, Mir, but thank you, thank you."

Mir exited the stairwell, declaring, "YOU HAVE TO BELIEVE!"

"Whew, made it just in time to get the last seat, art class was packed to the hilt," muttered Lars.

The room was used previously as a wood shop class, which was twice the size of a regular seating class. Forty students waited eagerly to delve into the arts. Two teachers were going to lead the class, one to instruct and one to assist. Each student was provided with canvas and painting materials.

"These instructions are pretty simple," Lars thought.

"Paint on your canvas anything that comes to mind," said the instructor. "This is a non- grading class strictly for expression. The final contest is to show expression and who does it best."

That was easy for Lars for he had nothing on his mind but the heirloom. He had to question if it was real. "What kind of magic is this? He does appear and disappear mysteriously," Lars puzzled to himself. "For it to work he said I have to believe."

The class was instructed to begin their painting by outlining.

Lars outlined the coin-shaped heirloom, though he hadn't had the chance to see it when Mir placed it in his pocket. He began to create on canvas how the heirloom would look, based on his expectations of what it looked like. He learned how to make a perfect circle. He painted the circle on his canvas the size of a volleyball. What came to mind then was mystical and mystery mysterioush—he thought of drawing an intricate maze in the circle.

Meanwhile his best friend, Shellmond, and his new friend, Tina, felt completely confident that their paintings were showing the talents of a potential winner, too.

Shellmond's outline was a giant hard roll sandwich with four inches of meat, vegetables and condiments inside. He needed some assistance to outline the hard roll sandwich. His idea was to use many colors to produce a psychedelic effect.

Tina was painting a stork with peacock feathers using only two colors, black and white.

Each student had help outlining their painting from the assistant. Each student paid close attention to their own creation. The details were essential.

Lunch period really didn't allow time to eat lunch, and participate in an art contest as well. For such a time-limited project, the class was given until the end of the month to complete their artwork, and get ready to compete with it.

The art instructor called out at the end of the first day, "Lunch is ending, we'll see you students tomorrow."

The bell sounded. The students moved back to class like stuffed cattle that grazed the mountainside. But Lars' step had a different power now. He looked energized feeding off the heirloom, feeling its powers.

# Chapter 17

# Lars Begins to Believe

During the last half of the school day, room 205 had its daily quiz. Shellmond couldn't believe how Lars was immersed in the quiz. Answering questions left and right, he had finished the quiz a lot sooner than usual.

Shellmond asked, "What has gotten into you this morning?"

"I don't know, I just feel good," smiled Lars.

Unbeknownst to Shellmond, the new revived Lars was a product of Mir the Magician's heirloom.

Lars guiltily thought, "It must stay classified that I was given this gift. If revealed it will lose its strength for the beholder. I wish I could give Shellmond one," he sighed.

Lars asked Shellmond, "Would you like to come to work with me?" Shellmond, without hesitation, agreed.

"Let's see if we can get a position for you at Biggs Grocery Store, Shellmond."

"Yes, I'm hoping for just that. I also would like to receive that same energy and focus you possess. Are you working out without me?"

"No, no way, my friend, as a matter of fact, today we can put together a routine and start tomorrow morning."

"You bet," exclaimed Shellmond.

Departing from the school premises, the boys headed for Biggs Grocery Store.

"Hello Lars," a Biggs Grocery Store clerk greeted him. "I see you brought a friend."

"Yep, he's going to help me if the manager allows it. All he must do is to sign the disclosure that Biggs are not responsible for any injuries, etc. It's what I signed," said Lars.

Soon they met with the manager, and Shellmond was cleared to work. It just so happened that it was a somewhat slow day, so Lars was able to show Shellmond the ropes uninterrupted.

Lars said, "Think about the personality, the respect and the patience you would want to have. People are already uptight so a smile with patience can bring a little comfort to the customers."

# Chapter 18

# Tackling Mr 'T'

As the end of their workday unfolded, the two gathered their belongings from the breakroom and proceeded home. All at once, Mr. 'T' appeared on the scene.

"Each of you boys made adequate tips today, how about a treat?"

Shellmond was first to feel the urge. Lars replied, "We decided to make changes you and I: fighting Mr. 'T', getting you a job, starting a workout schedule. We begin tomorrow. Can't let our guard down any longer."

"Wow, Lars, you have really kicked it into another gear, well I want to ride in that gear, too. Okay, let's do it. Let's walk right by those delicious Sophie Soft cupcakes and not look back," asserted Shellmond.

For the first time Lars licked Mr. 'T'. He finally won a battle, but the war was far from over.

Lars acquired a jolt of confidence and resilience. He was convinced it was the strength of the heirloom. Deep in conversation, they soon reached the intersection where they met each morning before school.

"Later, Lars, see you tomorrow, early."

"That's right," replied Lars.

They agreed to meet up at 5 am to walk a mile along with some calisthenics.

As he was washing up for dinner Lars noticed an unfamiliar table setting, a table for three. Mr. Pushkin's busy work schedule kept him away from the dinner table frequently. Sharing pleasantries over their meal, Lars began to tell them all that had happened to him.

His descriptions began with entering the art competition and that the class was held at lunch time. Gasping for air, Mr. Pushkin responded, "You are allowing a class to interfere with lunch? Something surely has your attention—I hope you use it to your benefit."

Lars went on about how much energy and focus he had acquired. Mr. Pushkin again interrupted. "How about using that newfound energy on the front yard? It's long overdue."

"No problem. Matter of fact, Shellmond and I start our new regimen of getting into shape tomorrow at 5 am."

"My goodness, I certainly like the sound of that," said Mr. Pushkin, as Mrs. Pushkin came over to serve Lars a second helping.

"No thank you, Mom." He declined the second serving.

"We also made a vow to curb our consumption. No more double dipping, ice cream cupcake slipping or calorie tripping, our minds are made up.

I even beat Mr. 'T' today."

"Who's Mr. 'T'?" asked Mr. Pushkin.

"He's the temptation that insists I eat sweets continuously while gaining unwanted weight, and I couldn't shake him until now. It's been a wonderful day today."

"Lars, we couldn't be any prouder."

That very morning before the sun was allowed to shine, Lars was up and at 'em. Their first task was to tackle the front yard. His idea was to use the yardwork as their first workout.

Lars bolted to meet Shellmond at their preferred street corner.

"Good morning Lars," Shellmond said as he approached his friend.

"Good morning to you, Shellmond. I came up with an idea for today's workout. 'Our front yard'."

Shellmond exhaled. "What, you think we can finish that before school?"

"We can try," proclaimed Lars. If we don't finish before it's time to leave for school, we can finish on the weekend. I promise I will be in your debt, Shellmond."

"Okay, Lars let's get to it," shouted Shellmond.

The boys went at it: cutting, raking, sweeping and trimming. Two hours passed.

Mrs. Pushkin yelled out, "BREAKFAST IS SERVED."

Their appetites had grown to where the boys felt like they could eat anything put in front of them. They had really worked hard—so hard that they had finished the job that should have taken a lot longer. Shellmond was still in awe at the way Lars was moving.

"What has gotten into you? You're practically running circles around me!"

"Well, Shellmond, I started a workout routine a week ago and so far, this is the result." What Lars really meant was that it had been on his mind a week ago to start a workout routine. Today was his real first day of exercising.

The boys cleaned up and sat at the table. Naturally, the table looked like the menu of one's favorite restaurant.

"Here we have another test, Shellmond." Lars began consciously placing small bites of delectable breakfast goodies in his mouth.

Shellmond followed Lars' lead. "Now we'll chew longer, taking smaller bites."

Mr. and Mrs. Pushkin were flabbergasted by what they were witnessing.

"You boys are downright serious about making a change for yourselves. It's uplifting and encouraging. Congratulations to you both," applauded an elated Mr. Pushkin.

Mrs. Pushkin added, "You two did a wonderful job in the front yard. Why, it looks like the work of landscapers. It's time for you two to hurry off to school, time is pressing."

On the way to school, they conversed about the art class held at lunch, as well as about Tina, Benny and Mr. 'T'.

"How are you feeling after breakfast this morning, Lars?"

"Totally energized, comfortable and not overstuffed. Hey, we have two blocks before the school grounds. Let's run!"

"Run?" Shellmond disputed his friend's sanity.

"Yeah, come on!"

Shellmond discreetly stifled a smile. "Okay, Lars."

Lars rubbed his chest where the coin pocket was stitched; in there was the heirloom. He took off running with a comfortable stride. He left

Shellmond a good way back, reaching the schoolyard first. Shellmond followed up in the rear, out of breath, bent over with his hands on his knees. The other students shot quick and curious glances at Lars.

Shellmond yelled, "You're not out of breath?"

"No," exclaimed Lars. "I feel like I could run another block."

The fact of the matter was, Lars didn't want to admit he might have pushed a little too hard. His body was in a bit of shock, unprepared for all the extra curriculum. The shock tapered off as Lars gathered himself, adjusting to the hellacious first day of workout and the recurring battle with Mr. 'T'.

The two friends glowed with pride at what they had accomplished that morning.

# Chapter 19

# Butting Heads with Benny

While there was still plenty of time before the first bell rang for class, a touch football game was about to start. Shellmond said, "Let's try to get picked to play, Lars." The two made themselves noticeable by waving their hands high in the air, as the teams were being sorted out.

By surprise, Shellmond and Lars were picked by different teams. Just as the game was about to begin, along came Benny.

"I'm playing, and someone's not!" yelled Benny, speaking to both squads.

As usual the smallest student that had been picked was forced to sit out. Benny took his place.

No one liked the idea, not even the team that Benny wanted to be on. chose. Though, Benny was a bigger kid and would be more capable to help win, it's the principle and Benny's move was unfair. It left a bad taste in all the players' mouths, especially Lars.

Finally, the game began. Lars was used mainly for blocking because of his size. Then he rubbed his chest to feel the heirloom, which was in the shape of a coin. He performed some fantastic blocks for his teammates, to the point where their team was the first to score.

What really caught everyone's eye, however, was how Lars was moving. He seemed very quick and agile for his size.

Both squads were also amazed by how Lars was blocking Benny the bully. He kept Benny from tagging the runner who scored.

Shellmond showed promise as well. He felt like his first day of workout had hurled him into another level of physicality.

Lars' team kicked off once again. Shellmond showed tenacity, running up front to accommodate his teammate with a block. That teammate was Benny. Benny ran through a couple of would-be defenders, running with the ball as if it were all too easy.

Suddenly, Benny was caught from behind, He was tagged by none other than Lars. The schoolyard erupted in shouts of joy. No one could believe what they had just observed, Lars caught Benny to tag him out.

Lars' team won! Just then, the school bell rang.

Everyone in school was talking about the game. In class, Lars was surrounded by his classmates asking him questions. They questioned him about his newfound energy and strength. "What's your new diet, your workout practice, your exercise plan?"

He had never felt like this, where people were acknowledging his existence and wanting to get to know him.

Shellmond talked with a couple of onlookers who saw a change in him as well.

Ms. Dunne ordered everyone to return to their seats and prepare themselves for today's lessons.

Lars' thoughts were now in a whirlwind. He quietly contemplated his successes.

"I'm sitting next to Tina, which she has chosen to do. I've had a battle or two with Mr. 'T' and won; I'm performing and completing things I never could before," he thought, as he rubbed his chest to feel the heirloom. "I chalk it up to Mir. He's given me hope with his heirloom. Clearly I must keep this a secret."

As lesson materials were being handed out, the students couldn't stop whispering about Lars catching Benny from behind to stop him from scoring.

Meanwhile, in Benny's class it was a different story.

Complete silence ruled that room. With that silence Benny was certain that the students had plenty to say about overweight Lars outrunning him. Yet all the students kept their comments to themselves.

Benny couldn't wait for lunchtime to confront Lars. On the other hand, Lars couldn't wait until lunch, either. He had his art class and competition to attend.

Snatching up what he could for lunch in the school cafeteria, Lars sprinted to art class. The students were showing more and more desire for their art composition. In their own minds they were creating masterpieces.

Lars' painting featured intricate patterns that amused the instructors, and they gave him accolades. Again, he rubbed his chest to absorb more power from the heirloom. "It's the heirloom that's offering me ideas for my painting," Lars assured himself.

Art class and lunch came to an end. Students rushed back to their classes for the last two hours of the school day.

Nothing sounds a sweeter note to students than when the last bell rings for the day.

Off to Biggs Grocery Store trudged Lars and Shellmond. Shellmond asked,

"You think work will pick up today?"

"Oh yeah, it seems, Shellmond, that Thursdays through Sundays are the busiest.

So, assemble your best manners, it will help you get better tips," smiled Lars.

"I heard today Benny was being Benny again at lunchtime. Probably embarrassed by you, he took it out on someone else. Then he interrupted a perfectly competitive kick ball game, and no one stopped him," shrugged Shellmond.

Nearing Biggs Grocery Store, Lars felt a wild, primitive explosion inside. Then he began to rub his chest saying to himself, "One of these days, Benny."

Reaching their destination, Lars and Shellmond viewed the packed parking lot. They looked at each other with a grin, gave a high five and began their song.

"Big tip day, big tip day, this will be a big tip day." Slipping on their aprons, they couldn't get them on fast enough. They were in demand.

The repeating customers loved Lars, and were touched by Shellmond's kindness.

They saw he was eager to agree to do anything they suggested. It was an obvious pleasure for him. It wasn't long before Shellmond was noted for his professionalism and kindness.

Just around quitting time, Lars was loading the last bag of groceries for an elderly couple when the aged gentleman fainted, falling backward. Lars was able to catch him. Gently lowering him to the ground, he screamed for Shellmond to call 911. Shellmond retrieved a phone from a bystander and called for an ambulance.

Shellmond ran for water and towels and brought them to Lars. Lars began massaging the old man's chest area with the towel doused in water. An employee passed Lars another towel. He placed the cool towel behind the elderly gentleman's neck. The ambulance arrived and the emergency crew took over what Lars and Shellmond had started.

Onlookers crowded around the scene. Curiosity filled the air; they all were nudging for the best view. In the midst of the situation stood Mir the Magician, unseen by Lars. Mir was thrilled to see Lars' progress in his transformation. The heirloom had awakened Lars.

The boys began to receive all sorts of recognition of a job well done.

Fading away from the crowd, Mir was spotted by Shellmond. He alerted Lars, "There's Mir the Magician." Lars, engaged in a conversation with a paramedic, halted and turned to Shellmond. "Where?"

Shellmond pointed, "Right there! Right—! Well, he was there, or it sure looked like him."

"I wonder why he was here," Lars pondered.

The crowd in the parking lot began to disperse. The elderly gentleman was taken to the emergency room. The elderly couple's neighbor happened to be there. They were able to take the man's elderly wife, car and groceries to their home.

Amid all this, Tina and her mom were grocery shopping and witnessed the whole episode. They walked over to Lars.

"I'm really impressed with your quick decision making. You literally saved a life today, young man."

"Thank you," replied Lars."

Tina interjected, "Mom, I would like you to meet my schoolmate, Lars."

"Pleased to meet you, Lars." He was overwhelmed with the introduction. His mind was spinning with thoughts of dating Tina.

Being tongue-tied, he replied, "Meased to pleet you." They all looked at him, then laughed. "I mean, pleased to meet you." Lars began to rub his chest. He needed a touch of courage; at that moment intimidation was lurking.

Lars was faced with an interesting possibility: "Tina could be more than just my friend, and her mom seems to like me." After the pleasantries and compliments, Lars departed from Tina and her mom to meet up with Shellmond.

Shellmond was also receiving compliments and acknowledgements of a fine job done today.

The manager of Biggs reached out specifically to the boys.

"What an advantage we have, with you two working here. When you've reached sixteen years of age, you'll have a real job waiting here for you both. You can break off early today, even though it's almost quitting time," he finished, chuckling.

Lars and Shellmond counted their tips. Immediately their eyes got big, trying to decide what they could buy to snack on.

# Chapter 20

# Taking Down Mr 'T'

Knock, knock. It was Mr. 'T' in his elegant attire. He started his rant. The boys stared down at the bakery shelf. Today's feature was Tasty Bites, newly baked bite-sized cupcakes made fresh daily at Biggs Grocery Store's bakery.

"Lars, are you going to partake of those Tasty Bites? They'll taste better then Sophie Soft cupcakes," Shellmond whispered persuasively.

Lars agreed that was a possibility. Sophie Soft cupcakes were prepacked, and filled with preservatives. On the other hand, Tasty Bites were baked daily here with no preservatives. Feeling weakness, Lars began to rub his chest where the heirloom lay.

"I've been noticing you lately rubbing your chest. It seems to happen right before you make a decision of some sort. Are you having chest pains?" Shellmond asked in a concerned voice.

"No, no pains," replied Lars. "It's just an old habit."

"I just don't remember you doing that. Ok, so with this tip money what would you like to try, what flavor is standing out to you the most?"

While Lars was rubbing his chest, Mr. 'T' was lurking, wanting Lars to give in to those tasty bites. Shellmond had already given in to Mr. 'T's demands.

Lars took a step back from the bakery shelves and condemned the Tasty Bites.

Mesmerized by Lars' firm decision, Shellmond joined in.

"Wow, Lars, you're bringing out the best in me. As for you, you're a new man!

I wouldn't believe it if I hadn't seen it. You are no longer showing the insecurities that kept you hopeless."

On the way home they talked about the ordeal at work: how people were calling them heroes for saving a life. It was indeed a harrowing position to be in.

"We handled it with professionalism and maturity," they congratulated themselves, giving each other the high five.

"See you tomorrow morning Lars, 5 am," said Sheldon proudly to his friend.

"5 am sharp, Shellmond." They headed for their homes.

The boys couldn't wait to get home to tell their families about what they had experienced at work that day. They both had their family's attention, intrigued with the details of how they were honored with the recognition of a fine deed.

Days turned into weeks. The end of the semester was coming up fast; the art class as well. During the art class, the students had come up with incredible paintings, including still life designs, animals, cities, mountainsides and other landscapes. Lars completed his intricate patterns that enhanced the heirloom shaped like a coin.

Today the instructors would select the two best paintings, then they would allow the students to choose the winner of the contest from those final two.

Rising to a promising sun-filled day, Lars went through his morning rituals preparing for school. Barreling out the door for school, Lars wished his parents a wonderful day.

Feeling unsettled, Mrs. Pushkin asked, "What about breakfast, Lars?"

"I'm running a little late. I have to meet Shellmond at the corner."

"You have to eat something before school."

"I am, Mom, I have a banana. That will keep me until lunch," Lars answered.

Almost passing out, she couldn't believe what she had heard.

"My boy is truly making a change for himself."

Thanks to Tina spreading the news at school the following day, Lars and Shellmond's names were buzzing all over the school. The administration went so far as to have a short assembly to congratulate the boys.

Lars and Shellmond were now gaining an advantage over Mr. 'T'. They had begun to win their battles conclusively against him.

# Chapter 21

# Lars Bests Benny

The two walked onto the schoolyard. Students were setting up A football game. Benny, making himself captain of a team, began to pick the players he wanted on his team. This time, Lars and Shellmond were teammates. Lars rubbed his chest, feeling the surge of power and confidence from the heirloom.

The first play of the game somehow Lars made an Interception and almost scored. The interception came because of a miscalculated throw from Benny. As the game went on, Lars' team was winning.

It became Lars' team after the interception.

Benny's team was having difficulty scoring due to Benny's lack of the "team player" attitude.

Lars' team got the ball back. Looking to score again, the ball was hiked to Shellmond. He began to run, using Lars' blocking to try to get into scoring position.

Benny charged down the field, looking furious, trying to tag Shellmond or worse. He was also jealous of the boys, because of how the school was making them out to be ideal peers and heroes.

Lars was now filled with courage. He knew Benny was going to explode. With a strong conviction, he smashed into Benny to block for Shellmond.

BLAM!" The sound of the collision filled the schoolyard. No one could believe their eyes, as Lars and Benny knocked each other down, while Shellmond shuffle-danced in to score. Then the bell rang to begin another school day.

Lars and Benny stared at each other. Benny had to think of something quick, to explain how he was knocked down. He had to maintain his persona that he was the king of the school. He lashed out, "I slipped when we blocked each other." No one wanted to hear that excuse, when they had seen Lars smack right into Benny and both of them fell down.

Lars got up, brushing himself off while chuckling about it. "No hard feelings, okay, Benny?"

Benny didn't take that comment lightly. In anger, he pushed Lars hard.

Lars didn't budge. "I don't want to fight, Benny, it was just a game." Benny didn't care. He slapped Lars across the face, leaving a handprint on Lars' cheek.

Once more, Lars rubbed his chest, then gave Benny a shove to knock him down. Benny got up slowly, as if he had been pushed by an action hero. The students in the schoolyard began to cheer for Lars, shaking his hands, patting him on his back, stating, "Lars is the man! He just stopped Benny. No one's ever stopped Benny till now."

Shellmond rushed over, grabbing Lars for class. "The bell has rung— we'll be late. Let's get going."

The class couldn't keep from talking about Lars smashing into Benny.

"I heard what happened, Lars," Tina replied.

"Yeah, I never had to respond to an action like that before. To be honest, I'm glad that's all it took, I don't like to fight."

"It seems he didn't either. When you pushed him down like that, you'd think he would retaliate. Lars, you surely have changed, and I like it," declared Tina.

Lars took a moment to assess the goals he had set for himself. His accomplishments began with combatting Mr. 'T' beating him at his own game, designing a better diet for himself, losing inches around his midsection, maintaining daily workout practices and finally going face to face with Benny.

Lars was really feeling like a winner.

All the students and staff were waiting to hear the results of the art contest. The art contest instructors said, "It has been narrowed down to work by two students: Lars' coin painting and Tina's bird painting. The winner will be decided tomorrow."

Lars and Tina were excited to have the best two paintings.

During lunchtime, the atmosphere in the school was different. Students were walking around with their lunches in hand as if to dare Benny to react like before. Lars' confrontation with Benny obviously gave hope to others not to be afraid to stand up for their rights.

Benny sensed the newfound fearlessness that was circulating through the school. He stayed neutral and decided to work on his attitude and character. He now stood alone with no followers, no intimidated students to bully. Benny decided he wanted to be a better person.

After a full day at school and work, Lars returned home. Hastily he took his school clothes off to jump in the shower. It had been a long and wonderful day.

Astonished about the power of the heirloom, Lars went over and over in his head how he had gained power to combat Mr. 'T' and defeated him.

"As well, I'm winning with my new diet. I even have my parents eating healthier. I've won there. I've gotten over my intimidation by Benny. I have a great friend now who's a girl, I never had that before," he congratulated himself.

"Wow, that heirloom is real. I hope Mir the Magician doesn't ask for it back.

Then maybe I can let Shellmond use it for a while." Enjoying his long hot shower,

Lars was mesmerized about how the day had played out and his life in general.

Mrs. Pushkin was gathering clothes to do the laundry. She entered each room to find clothes that needed washing. "Lars' clothes need it the most," she thought, "especially that hoodie."

After his long hot shower, Lars dried himself off, then dressed in loose lounging clothes for comfort.

Unexpectedly, there was a phone call. It was the art instructor calling to congratulate Lars as the winner of the art contest

"The students chose your painting, Lars," revealed the instructor. Lars stammered, "Thank you so much!" and hung up the phone. Jumping up and down for joy, not sounding so loud this time now that he's lost so much weight and inches. He ran up and down the hallway with sheer delight.

He stopped to touch his chest, wanting to rub the heirloom—and noticed he wasn't wearing his hoodie. At that time, he heard the washing machine and dryer clamor. Nervousness set in. Lars bolted to his room and noticed the clothes that he had worn that day were gone. He knew where they were, in the washer and dryer. Lars began to tremble with fear that the heirloom would be dislodged from the hoodie.

"Mir said it couldn't be moved once it was in the coin pocket of my hoodie," remembered Lars, stunned with disbelief that he had left the hoodie unattended to be washed. Shaking like a timid homeless kitten, he was sure he was going to lose all the power from the heirloom once it fell out of the coin pocket.

He stopped the washer to look for his hoodie. It wasn't there; he checked the dryer.

"Oh boy, my hoodie," he sighed in relief. He grabbed it like a security blanket and felt for the heirloom, but didn't find it. Now he was really bothered. He searched the dryer diligently. Finally, at the end of his stretched fingers, he touched it.

"Got it, " he said, and grabbed the coin.

The heirloom turned out to be simply a quarter. "A quarter—just a twenty-five cent coin," he said to himself in amazement. He looked repeatedly in the washer and dryer, and concluded there never was an heirloom. "It was always a quarter. Mir tricked me. I did this all on my own!"

"Maybe Mir saw my potential; he just figured out a way to bring it out. Mir taught me how to believe—in myself."

"I'M A WINNER!" shouted Lars.

CPSIA information can be obtained
at www.ICGtesting.com
Printed in the USA
BVHW080034070721
611238BV00016B/996

9 780228 858089